This Orchard book
belongs to

....
....
....

For Oliver and Ellie

ORCHARD BOOKS
338 Euston Road, London NW1 3BH
Orchard Books Australia
Level 17/207 Kent Street, Sydney, NSW 2000
First published in 2014 by Orchard Books
First paperback publication in 2015
ISBN 978 1 40833 137 8
Text © Jerome Keane 2014
Illustrations © Susana de Dios 2014
The rights of Jerome Keane to be identified as the author and of Susana de Dios to be identified as
the illustrator of this book have been asserted by them in accordance with the Copyright,
Designs and Patents Act, 1988.
A CIP catalogue record for this book is available from the British Library.
1 3 5 7 9 10 8 6 4 2
Printed in China
Orchard Books is a division of Hachette Children's Books, an Hachette UK company.
www.hachette.co.uk

Jerome Keane & Susana de Dios

MINE!

ORCHARD

Fox was bored.

Horse was bored.

Nothing had happened for ages.

But then something did . . .

Fox noticed.
Horse noticed.

Horse pretended he hadn't seen.
Fox pretended he hadn't seen.

But they were both thinking
the same thing . . .

"IT'S

MINE!”

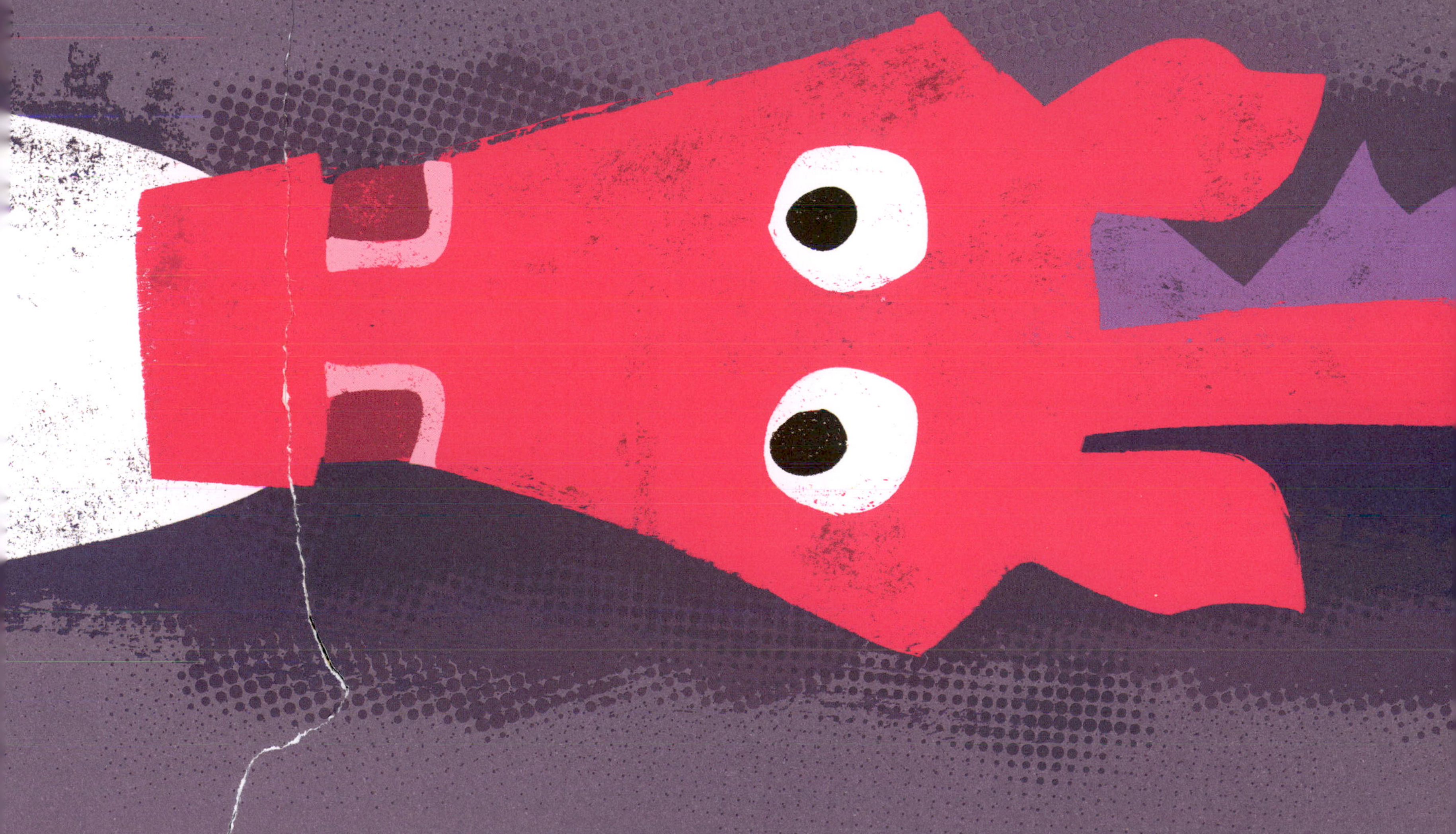

"That thing belongs to ME," said Horse.

"No, that thing belongs to ME," said Fox.

"But I saw it first," said Horse.
"No, it's mine," said Fox. "I saw it first."

"Didn't,"
said Horse.

"Did,"
said Fox.

"You really didn't," said Horse.
"Really did," said Fox.

Oh dear, this
was getting them
nowhere . . .

"Okay," said Horse.
"How about I play with it
first over HERE . . .

. . . and YOU wait
over THERE?"

"Or . . . I play first over HERE," said Fox, "and you wait over THERE?"

"Hang on," said Horse. "If you're right THERE and I'm right HERE, we may as well play at the same time."

"You mean play TOGETHER?"
asked Fox. "KIND OF SHARING?"

"Uh-oh . . ."

Fox was sad.
Horse was sad.

But then another
thing happened . . .

And this time it was going
to be different . . .

"This is nice," said Horse.
"Er, yes," said Fox. "It's good to share."